Adventures with Grandpa!

By Tex Huntley
Illustrated by Fabrizio Petrossi

 A GOLDEN BOOK • NEW YORK

T#: 555759

rhcbooks.com

ISBN 978-1-5247-6874-4

Printed in the United States of America

10 9 8 7 6 5 4 3 2 1

One day, Ryder and the PAW Patrol were at Mr. Porter's market and restaurant with their friend Alex. Mr. Porter was Alex's grandpa—or, as Alex liked to call him, "the best grandpa ever!"

"I have a special treat for all of you today!" Mr. Porter announced.

"What is it?" Alex asked, jumping up and down excitedly.

Chase took a deep whiff with his super sniffer. "My nose knows! It's cherry pie!"

"And cherry pup treats for the PAW Patrol!"
said Mr. Porter as he served Alex and the team.
"I could never forget our favorite pups!"
He headed back into his restaurant.
    "This is yummy in my tummy!" said Rubble,
licking his lips. "Mr. Porter is such a great baker."
    "And a great grandpa, too!" Alex added.

"We should do something nice for him," Zuma suggested.

"That's a super idea," said Ryder. "What do you think he'd like?"

Alex and the pups thought for a moment.

"Well, he likes to cook," Alex said.
"Yeah!" said Skye. "Remember the pizza party in the mountains?"

"But we almost didn't get there!" Alex recalled. "We were bringing the pizza dough to the party when our delivery truck hit a patch of ice. We nearly slid off the road!"

"That's when I zoomed to the rescue with my copter!" Skye said, remembering. "I lowered the harness . . ."

". . . and I buckled in and became Super Alex!" he cheered.

Then Chase pulled the truck back onto the road with his winch. Mr. Porter was glad the pizza ingredients and the truck were safe, but he was even happier that Alex was safe!

"Mr. Porter loves helping you do new things, Alex," Rocky said. "Remember the time he helped you make your Super Trike?"

"You guys built the Super Trike using items from the restaurant," Rocky went on. "There was a vegetable crate for a seat and big trays for wheels. Mr. Porter really knows how to reuse and recycle!"

"He taught me everything I know," Alex said proudly.

"And your grandpa likes to go hiking with you," Rubble reminded him.

"That's true," Alex said. "We hike in the woods all the time!"

"Once, when we were hiking," said Alex, "Grandpa sat in a hollow stump and got stuck! It's a good thing we can always count on you pups!"

"You know it!" Zuma said. "Whenever you need us, just yelp for help!"

Remembering all the wonderful adventures with his grandpa gave Alex an idea.

"What if we had a surprise party for my grandpa?" he said. "Do you think he'd like that?"

"Yes!" Ryder said. "And the PAW Patrol can help you do it! Let's roll!"

Marshall helped Skye make a big banner for the party.

"Water cannons ready!" Marshall announced. He used them to squirt paint onto a long sheet.

When it was dry, Skye took it to her helicopter.

After that, Alex worked with Ryder and
the rest of the pups on a very special pizza.
"Let's make it *pup*-peroni," said Rubble
with a giggle.

While the pups drove the food and decorations to the woods, Alex asked his grandpa to go for a hike.

Mr. Porter thought for a moment. "Well, I was just about to close the market, and—"

Alex grabbed his grandpa's hand. "Great! Let's go!"

After they changed into hiking clothes, Alex and his grandpa headed into the forest.

"It's great being with you, Alex," Mr. Porter said.

"I love all the time we spend together, Grandpa," Alex said. "That's why I have a surprise for you. . . ."

The two rounded a bend and found Ryder and the pups waiting with the party all set up.

"Surprise!" they cried.

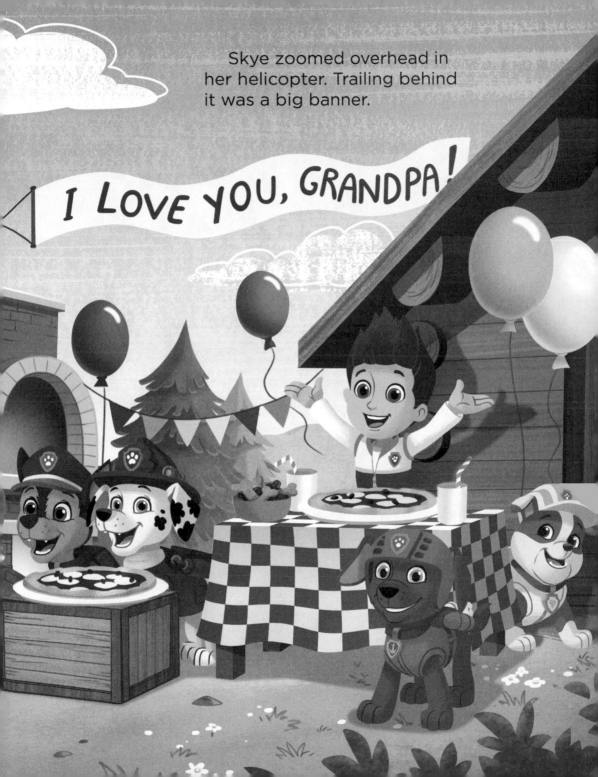

Skye zoomed overhead in her helicopter. Trailing behind it was a big banner.

I LOVE YOU, GRANDPA!

Mr. Porter was very surprised. He couldn't believe everyone had done this for him. And he was especially surprised by the pizza—it looked like him!

"It's Grandpa-face pizza!"
Alex cheered.

"Alex, thank you for such a wonderful party," Mr. Porter said. "But you didn't need to do all this. Having you as a grandson is the only gift I need."

"You're the best grandpa ever!" Alex said, giving him a big hug.

Adventures with the PAW Patrol were great, but Alex couldn't wait for the next adventure with his grandpa.